Rosemary

A Christmas Story

A. M. Williamson, C. N. Williamson

Alpha Editions

This edition published in 2023

ISBN : 9789357940344

Design and Setting By
Alpha Editions
www.alphaedis.com
Email - info@alphaedis.com

Contents

Evelyn and Rosemary climbed hand in hand, while Hugh carried the
two huge baskets.

THE WHITE GIRL ON THE TERRACE: THE ROSE GIRL AT THE CASINO

There was a young man in Monte Carlo. He had come in a motor car, and he had come a long way, but he hardly knew why he had come. He hardly knew in these days why he did anything. But then, one must do something.

It would be Christmas soon, and he thought that he would rather get it over on the Riviera than anywhere else, because the blue and gold weather would not remind him of other Christmases which were gone—pure, white, cold Christmases, musical with joy-bells and sweet with aromatic pine, the scent of trees born to be Christmas trees.

There had been a time when he had fancied it would be a wonderful thing to see the Riviera. He had thought what it would be like to be a rich man, and bring a certain girl here for a moon of honey and roses.

She was the most beautiful girl in the world, or he believed her so, which is exactly the same thing; and he had imagined the joy of walking with her on just such a terrace as this Casino terrace where he was walking now, alone. She would be in white, with one of those long ermine things that women call stoles; an ermine muff (the big, "granny" kind that swallows girlish arms up to the dimples in their elbows) and a hat which they would have bought together in Paris.

They would have bought jewels, too, in the same street where they found the hat; the Rue de la Paix, which she had told him she longed to see. And she would be wearing some of the jewels with the white dress—just a few, not many, of course. A string of pearls (she loved pearls) a swallow brooch (he had heard her say she admired those swallow brooches, and he never forgot anything she said); with perhaps a sapphire-studded buckle on her white suéde belt. Yes, that would be all, except the rings, which would lie hidden under her gloves, on the dear little hands whose nails were like enamelled rose leaves.

When she moved, walking beside him on the terrace, there would be a mysterious silky whisper and rustle, something like that you hear in the woods, in the spring, when the leaves are crisp with their pale green youth, and you shut your eyes, listening to the breeze telling them the secrets of life.

There would be a fragrance about the white dress and the laces, and ermine, and the silk things that you could not see,—a fragrance as mysterious as the rustling, for it would seem to belong to the girl, and not to have come from any bottle, or bag of sachet powder. A sweet, fresh, indefinable fragrance, like the smell of a tea rose after rain.

They would have walked together, they two, and he would have been so proud of her, that every time a passer-by cast a glance of admiration at her face, he would feel that he could hardly keep in a laugh of joy, or a shout, "She is mine—she is mine."

But he had been poor in the old days, when from far away he had thought of this terrace, and the moon of honey and roses, and love. It had all been a dream, then, as it was now; too sweet ever to come true.

He thought of the dream, and of the boy who had dreamed it, half bitterly, half sadly, on this his first day in the place of the dream.

He was rich—as rich as he had seen himself in the impossible picture, and it would have been almost too easy to buy the white dress, and the ermine, and the pearls. But there was no one for whom he would have been happy to buy them. The most beautiful girl in the world was not in his world now; and none other had had the password to open the door of his heart since she had gone out, locking it behind her.

"She would have liked the auto," he said to himself. And then, a moment later, "I wonder why I came?"

It was a perfect Riviera day. Everybody in Monte Carlo who was not in the Casino was sauntering on the terrace in the sun; for it was that hour before luncheon when people like to say, "How do you do?—How nice to meet you here!" to their friends.

The young man from far away had not, so far as he knew, either enemies or friends at Monte Carlo. He was not conscious of the slightest desire to say "How do you do?" to any of the pretty people he met, although there is a superstition that every soul longs for kindred souls at Christmas time.

He had not been actively unhappy before he left the Hotel de Paris and strolled out on the terrace, to have his first sight of Monte Carlo by daylight. Always, there was the sore spot in his heart, and often it ached almost unbearably at night, or when the world hurt him with its beauty, which he must see without Her; but usually he kept the spot well covered up; and being healthy as well as young, he had cultivated that kind of contentment which Thoreau said was only desperate resignation in disguise. He took an interest in books, in politics, and sport and motor cars, and a good many other things; but on the terrace, the blue of the sea; the opal lights on the mountains; the gold glint of oranges among green, glittering leaves; the pearly glimmer of white roses thrown up like a spray against the sky, struck at his heart, and made the ache come back more sharply than it had for a long time.

If he had been a girl, tears would have blinded his eyes; but being what he was, he merely muttered in anger against himself, "Hang it all, what a wretched ass I am," and turning his back on the sea, made his way as fast as he could into the Casino.

It was close upon twelve o'clock, and the "Rooms" had been open to the public for two hours. The "early gamblers" thronging the Atrium to wait till the doors opened, had run in and snatched seats for themselves at the first tables, or marked places to begin at eleven o'clock, if crowded away from the first. Later, less ardent enthusiasts had strolled in; and now, though it was not by any means the "high season" yet, there were rows of players or lookers on, three deep round each table.

The young man was from the South—though a South very different from this. He had the warm blood of Virginia in his veins, and just so much of the gambler's spirit as cannot be divided from a certain recklessness in a man with a temperament. He had seen plenty of life in his own country, in the nine years since he was twenty, and he knew all about roulette and *trente et quarante*, among other things desirable and undesirable.

Still, gambling seemed to be made particularly fascinating here, and he wanted to be fascinated, wanted it badly. He was in the mood for the heavy hush of the Rooms, for the closeness, and the rich perfumes, which mingling together seem like the smell of money piled on the green tables; he was in a mood for the dimmed light like dull gold, gold sifted into dust by passing through many hands.

He had got his ticket of admission to the Casino, after arriving yesterday evening; but the Rooms had not pleased him then. He had not played, and had merely walked through, looking at the people; but now he went to a *trente et quarante* table, and reaching over the shoulders of the players—not so many as in the roulette rooms,—he put a five hundred franc note on *couleur*. It won. He let the money lie, and it won again. A third time and a fourth he left the notes on, and still luck was with him. He was in for a good run.

As it happened, nobody else had been playing higher than *plaques*, the handsome hundred franc gold pieces coined for the Principality of Monaco; and people began to watch the new comer, as they always do one who plays high and is lucky. On the fifth deal he had won the maximum. He took off half, and was leaving the rest to run, when a voice close to his shoulder said, "Oh, do take it all off. I feel it's going to lose now. To please *me*."

He took off half, and was leaving the rest to run, when a voice close to his shoulder said, "Oh, do take it all off."

—*Rosemary.*

He glanced aside, and saw an exceedingly pretty, dark face, which looked vaguely familiar. With a smile, he took up all the notes, and only just in time. Couleur lost; inverse won.

"Oh, I'm so glad," said the owner of the pretty face. She spoke English with a slight, but bewitching foreign accent; and her eyes shone at him like brown jewels under the tilted brim of a hat made all of pink and crimson roses. She was rather like a rose, too, a rich, colourful, spicy rose, of the kind which unfolds early. He knew that he had seen her before, and wondered where.

After all, it was rather nice to be spoken to by someone other than a hotel manager or a waiter; someone who was good to look at, and friendly. He lost interest in the game, and gained interest in the girl.

"Thank you," said he. "You've brought me luck."

"I hope you don't think I speak always to strangers, like that," said the girl in the rose hat. "But you see, I recognized you at once. I don't know if you remember me? No, I'm afraid you don't."

"Of course I remember you, only I can't think where we—"

"Why, it was in Paris. You saved my mother's little dog from being run over one day. We were both so grateful. Afterwards we saw you once or twice at tea at the Ritz, and you took off your hat, so you must have remembered then. Ah me, it's a long time ago!"

"Not so very," said the young man. "I remember well, now." (He wished her mother had not been quite such an appalling person, fat and painted.) "It was only last October. I'd just come to Paris. It was my first day there, when I picked up the little dog. Now, on my first day here, you pay me back for what I did then—as if it needed paying back!—by making me pick up my money. That's quite a coincidence."

They had moved away from the tables now, and were walking very slowly down the room. The young man smiled at the girl, as he crushed up the notes and stuffed them into his pocket. He saw that she was much prettier than he had thought her in Paris, if he had thought of her at all; and her dress of pale pink cloth was charming with the rose hat. Somehow, he was glad that she was not in white—with an ermine stole.

"So it is, quite a coincidence, and a pleasant one for me, since I meet again one who was once so kind," she said. "Especially it is good to meet a friend— if I may call you a friend?—when one is very sad."

"Of course you may call me a friend," said he, kindly. "I'm sorry to hear you are sad."

"That is why I told you the other meeting seemed a long time ago," explained the girl. "I was happy then. Now, I am breaking my heart, and I do not know what to do. Oh, I ought not to talk like this, for after all, you are a stranger. But you are English, or you are American; and men of those countries never misunderstand a woman, even if she is in trouble. We can feel ourselves safe with them."

"I'm American," he answered, "and I'm glad you feel like that. I wish I could help you in some way." He spoke kindly, but not with absolute warmth of sincerity. The girl saw this, and knew that he did not believe in her as she wished him to believe, as she intended to make him believe.

She looked up at him with sad and eloquent eyes, which softened his heart in spite of himself. "You can't help me, thank you," she said, "except by kind words and kind thoughts. I think, though, that it would do me good to tell you things, if you really take an interest?"

"Of course I do." He was speaking the truth now. He was human, and she was growing prettier, as she grew more pathetic, every moment.

"And would you advise me a little? I have nobody else to ask. My mother and I know no one at Monte Carlo. Perhaps you would walk with me on the terrace and let me talk?"

"Not on the terrace," he said, quickly, for he could not bear to meet the sweet ghost of the past in the white dress and ermine stole, as he gave advice to the flesh and blood reality of the present, in the pink frock and roses. "What about Ciro's? Couldn't we find your mother somewhere, and get her to chaperon us for lunch? I should think it must be very jolly now, in the Galerie Charles Trois."

"So it would be; but my poor mother is very ill in her bed," said the girl.

"Would she—er—do you think, as I'm an American, and we're almost old friends, mind letting you have lunch just with me alone? Of course, if she would mind, you must say no. But I must confess, I'm hungry as a wolf; and it would be somewhere to sit and talk together, quietly, you know."

"You are hungry," echoed the girl. "Ah, I would wager something that you don't really know what hunger is. But I know—now."

"What do you mean?"

"I mean it is well my mother is ill, and doesn't wish to eat, for there would be nothing for her, if she did."

"Good heavens! And you?"

"I have had nothing to eat since yesterday morning, and then only a biscuit with a glass of water."

"My poor girl, we won't say anything more about chaperons. Come along with me to Ciro's this instant, to lunch, and tell me everything."

He was completely won over now, and looked very handsome, with a slight flush on his brown face, and his dark eyes bright with excitement.

The girl lowered her long lashes, perhaps to hide tears.

When she did this, and drooped the corners of her mouth, she was very engaging, and the young man tingled all over with pity. That poor, pretty creature, starving, in her charming pink dress and hat of roses. How strange life was! It was something to be thankful for that he had met her.

A little while ago, he had walked through the Galerie Charles Trois, thinking how delightful the tables looked at Ciro's, and making up his mind to return there for lunch. But afterwards, on the terrace, he had been so miserable that he would probably have forgotten all about his plan, if it had not been for the girl.

Now, he chose a small table in a corner of the balcony, close to the glass screen. A month later, he might have had to engage it long beforehand; but to-day, though the place was well filled with pretty women and their attendant men, there was not a crowd, and he could listen to his companion's low-voiced confidences without fear of being overheard.

THE ROSE GIRL'S LITTLE STORY, AND GREAT EYES

He ordered a lunch which he thought the girl would like, with wine to revive the faculties that he knew must be failing. Then, when she had eaten a little, daintily in spite of her hunger, he encouraged her to talk.

"Mother and I are all alone in the world," she said. "We are Belgian, and live in Brussels, but we have drifted about a good deal, just amusing ourselves. Somehow we never happened to come here until a month ago. Then my mother said one day in Paris, 'Let us go to Monte Carlo. I dreamed last night that I won twenty thousand francs there.' My mother is rather superstitious. We came, and she did win, at first. She was delighted, and believed in her dream, so much that when she began to lose, she went up and up, doubling each time. They call the game she made, 'playing the martingale!'

"She lost all the money we had with us, and telegraphed home for more. Soon, she had sold out every one of our securities. Then she won, and went half mad with the joy and excitement, but the joy didn't last long. She lost all, again—literally, our all. We were penniless. There was nothing left to pay the hotel bill. I went out, and found a *Mont de Pieté*, just beyond the limits of the Principality; they aren't allowed inside. I pawned all our jewellery, and as we had a great many valuable things, I got several thousand francs. I thought the money would last us until I could find something to do. But, without telling me what she meant to do, mother took it all to the Casino—and—it followed the rest.

"She was so horrified at what she had done, when it was too late, that she wished to kill herself. It was a terrible time for me, but I was so sorry—so sorry for her."

As the girl said this, she looked full into the young man's eyes, with her great, appealing ones. He thought that she must have a wonderfully sweet nature, to have forgiven that horrible, fat old woman, after being subjected to so much undeserved suffering. It was a thousand pities, he said to himself, that a really good sort of girl should be forced to live her life beside a creature of that type, and under such an influence. He had not quite believed in the poor child, at first, perhaps, and because he did believe in her now, he felt poignant remorse for his past injustice.

"What did you do, then?" he asked, honestly absorbed in the story, for he was a generous and warm hearted fellow, who found most of his pleasure, in these latter days, in the help he could give others, to make them happier than he was himself.

"I comforted her as well as I could, but I didn't know what would become of us. Then a lady, who had a room next to mine in the hotel, heard me crying, and was very kind."

"I should think she would have been," interrupted the young man.

"She told me that, as my mother had lost everything, she had better go to the Direction of the Casino, and get what they call a viatique—money to go away with. So she did ask, though it was a great ordeal to make up her mind to do it; and they gave my mother a thousand francs. Then, you know, she had no right to play in the Rooms again; she was supposed to pay her hotel bill, and leave Monte Carlo. But she gave half the money to a woman she had met in the Rooms, and asked her to put it on six numbers she had dreamed about; she was sure that this time she would win."

"And did she?"

"No. The money was lost. We hadn't enough left to settle our account at the hotel, or to get away from the place, even if there were anywhere to go— when one has no pennies. So my mother begged me to slip into the Rooms, with what was left, and try to get something back. I had been trying when you saw me, with our last louis. Now you know why it seemed so good to see a man I knew, a face I could trust. Now you know why I, who had had such misfortunes, was glad at least to bring you luck."

"It's my turn to bring you some, I think," began the man she could trust; but she stopped him by putting up her plump little white hand.

"If you mean with money, no," she said, with soft decision that was pretty and sad to hear. "If you mean with advice, yes. If you could only get me something to do! You see, they will be turning us out of our hotel to-morrow. They've let us keep our rooms on, up to now, but for two days they've not given us anything to eat. Of course, it can't go on like this. If it hadn't been for you, I think when I went back to tell my mother that the last louis of the viatique was gone, we would have killed ourselves."

"Great Heaven, you must promise me not to do that," the young man implored.

"I will promise, now, for you have saved me by—caring a little. You do care, really, don't you?"

"I wouldn't have blood in my veins, if I didn't. But—about something for you to do—I must think."

"Are you staying here for some time?" asked the girl.

"I haven't made up my mind."

"I asked because I—I suppose you don't need a secretary, do you? I can write such a good English hand; and I know French and Italian as well as I do German, and your own language. If I could be of use, I would work so hard for you."

"I dare say I shall be needing a secretary after Christmas, indeed, I'm sure I shall," insisted the young man, more and more earnest in his desire to do good. "I have dozens of letters to write every day, and all sorts of odds and ends to keep straight. I could bring the things down to your place and you could help me, if you would. But I'm afraid it would be no end of bother to you."

"I should love it," said the girl, gently.

"Oh, it would be hard work. It would take a lot of your time, and be worth a lot of money."

"Would it really? But you mustn't overpay me. I should be so angry if you did that."

"There's no danger. I'm a good business man, I assure you. I should pay a capable secretary like you—knowing several languages and all that—say forty dollars a week. That's about two hundred francs."

"Wouldn't that be too much?"

"Hardly enough."

"You are so good—so good! But I knew you would be. I wonder if you would think me a very bold girl if I told you something? It's this; I've never forgotten you since those days in Paris. You were different, somehow, from other men I had seen. I thought about you. I had a presentiment that we should meet again. My mother dreamed of numbers to play at roulette. I dreamed of—but oh, I am saying things I ought not to say! Please don't blame me. When you've starved for two days, and not known what to do—unless to die, and then a man comes who is kind, and saves you from terrible things, you can't be as wise and well behaved as at other times."

"Poor child," said the young man.

"It does me good to be called that. But you don't know my name, the name of your new secretary. It is Julie—Julie de Lavalette. My mother is the Comtesse de Lavalette. And you?"

"Oh, I'm plain Hugh Egerton," said the young man.

The girl laughed. "I do not think you are plain Hugh Egerton at all. But perhaps an American girl would not tell you that? Hugh! What a nice name. I think it is going to be my favourite name."

She glanced up at him softly, under long lashes,—a thrilling glance; but he missed its radiance, for his own eyes were far away. Hugh had been the favourite name of another girl.

When she saw that look of his, she rose from her chair. "I'm taking too much of your time," she exclaimed, remorsefully. "I must go."

His eyes and thoughts came back to the wearer of pink and roses. Perhaps there had been just a little too much softness and sweetness. It had been wise of her to change the key, and speak of parting.

He paid for the lunch, and tipped the waiters so liberally that they all hoped he would come again often. Then he asked if he might walk with her to the hotel where she and her mother were staying.

"It's down in the Condamine," she hesitated. "We've moved there lately, since the money began to go, and we've had to think of everything. It's rather a long walk from here."

"All the better for me," he answered, and her smile was an appreciation of the compliment.

They sauntered slowly, for there was no haste. Nobody else wanted Hugh Egerton's society, and he began to believe that this girl sincerely did want it. He also believed that he was going to do some real good in the world, not just in the ordinary, obvious way, by throwing about his money, but by being genuinely necessary to someone.

When they had strolled down the hill, and had followed for a time the straight road along the sea on that level plain which is the Condamine, the girl turned up a side street. "We live here," she said, and stopped before a structure of white stucco, rococco decoration, and flimsy balconies. Large gold letters, one or two of which were missing, advertised the house as the Hotel Pension Beau Soleil; and those who ran might read that it would be charitable to describe its accommodation as second rate.

"It is not nice," she went on, with a shrug of her pretty shoulders. "But—it is good to know all the same that we will not be turned out. I have a new heart in my breast, since I left this house a few hours ago—because there is a You in the world."

As she said this, she held out her hand for goodbye, and when he had shaken it warmly, the young man was bold enough to slip off her wrist the little pink leather bag which hung there by its chain.

"Now for that advance on your secretarial work," he said; and taking from his pocket a wad of notes which he had won at the Casino, he stuffed it hastily into the yawning mouth of the bag, while the girl's soft eyes gazed at the sea. Then he closed the spring with a snap, and she let him pass the chain over her hand once more.

"Oh, but it looks very fat," she exclaimed. "Are you sure you counted right?"

"There's a little more there," he said, uncomfortably, "just a little to save the bother of counting here in the street. Don't look angry. Only the salary part's for you, of course, but the rest—couldn't you just hand it over to your mother, and say, 'Winnings at the Casino'? That's true, you know; it was, every bit. And you needn't say who won it. Besides, if it hadn't been for you, it would have been lost instead of won. It would be a kind of Christmas present for your mother from the Casino, which really owes her a lot more."

The girl shook her head, gently. "I couldn't do that, even for my mother's sake; but I don't misunderstand, now we are such friends. I know how kindly you mean, and though neither mother nor I can accept presents of money, even from dear friends (after all we are of the noblesse!) I'm not going to hurt you by giving the money back, if you will do what I ask of you."

"What is that?" He felt ready to do anything within reason.

"Let us sell you our dear little dog, for this extra money you have put into my bag. He is very, very valuable, for he cost thousands of francs, the sweet pet, so you would really have something not unworthy, in return for your goodness. Ah, don't say no. You would love Papillon, and we should love you to have him. We couldn't have parted with our little darling to a stranger, though we were starving; but it would make us happy to think he was yours. And then, if you won't, you must take all this back." As she spoke, she touched the bag on her arm.

"Oh, I'll have the dog!" Hugh Egerton said, quickly. Anything rather than the girl should return the money, which she so much needed. "I remember he was a dear little chap, Pomeranian or something of the sort. I hope he likes motors."

"He will like whatever you like. If you will come and fetch him this evening, I will show you all his tricks. Do come. It would be good to see you again so soon."

"With pleasure," said the young man, flushing slightly. "If you think your mother will be well enough to receive me?"

"The news I have to give will almost cure her. If you would dine with us? They will give us a dinner, now"—and she laughed childishly—"when I have paid the bill. It will be very stupid for you at a place like this, but you will have a welcome, and it is the best we can do."

"It is the welcome I want," said Hugh. "But if you and your mother could dine with me somewhere—"

"Another time we will."

There were to be other times, of course!

"And this evening," she went on, "we can talk of my beginning work, as your secretary. It shall be directly after Christmas?"

"Whenever you are ready."

"I suppose you have friends to whom you will go for Christmas?"

"Not a friend."

"Oh, perhaps we might be together—all three?"

"I'll think of something pleasant for us to do, if you'll let me."

"How good you are! Then, till this evening. It will seem long till then."

They shook hands once more. She had taken off her glove now, and her palm left on his a reminiscence of Peau d'Espagne. He did not know what the scent was, but it smelled rich and artificial, and he disliked to associate it with his new friend. "But probably it's her mother's, and she didn't choose it herself," he thought. "Well—I have a new interest in life now. I expect this is the best thing that's happened to me for a long time."

As he walked back to his hotel, his head was full of plans for the girl's transient pleasure and lasting benefit. "Poor lonely child," he thought. "And what a mother! She ought not to be left with a person like that. She ought to marry. It would be a good deed to take her away from such an influence. So young, and so ingenuous as she is still, in spite of the surroundings she must have known, she is capable of becoming a noble woman. Perhaps, if she turns out to be really as sweet and gentle as she seems—"

The sentence broke off unfinished, in his mind, and ended with a great sigh.

There could be only second best, and third best things in life for him now, since love was over, and it would be impossible for him to care for an angel from heaven, who had not the face and the dear ways of the girl he had lost. But second best things might be better than no good things at all, if only one made up one's mind to accept them thankfully. And it was a shame to waste so much money on himself, when there were soft-eyed, innocent girls in the world who ought to be sheltered and protected from harm.

WHEN THE CURTAIN WAS DOWN

The soft-eyed, innocent girl who had inspired the thought went into the hotel, and was rather cross to the youthful concierge, because the *ascenseur* was not working. There were three flights of stairs to mount before she reached her room, and she was so anxious to open her bag to see what was inside, that she ran up very fast, so fast that she stepped on her dress and ripped out a long line of gathers. Her eyes were not nearly as soft as they had been, while she picked up the hanging folds of pink cloth, and went on.

The narrow corridor at the top of the staircase was somewhat dark, and, her eyes accustomed to the brilliant light out of doors, the girl stumbled against a child who was coming towards her.

"*Petit bête!*" she snapped. "You have all but made me fall. Awkward little thing, why don't you keep out of people's way?"

The child flushed. She would have liked to answer that it was Mademoiselle who had got in her way; but Mother wished her to be always polite. "I am sorry," she replied instead, not saying a word about the poor little toes which the pretty pink lady had crushed.

"Well, then, if you are sorry, why don't you let me pass?" asked the girl of the soft eyes.

"If you please, I want to give you a note," said the child, anxiously searching a small pocket. "It's from Mother, for Madame. She told me to take it to your door; so I did, several times, but nobody answered. Here 'tis, please, Mademoiselle."

Mademoiselle snatched it from the hand, which was very tiny, and pink, with dimples where grown up folk have knuckles. She then pushed past the child, and went on to a door at the end of the passage, which she threw open, without knocking.

"*Eh bien*, Julie! You have been gone long enough to break the bank twice over. What luck have you had?" exclaimed the husky voice of a woman who sat in an easy chair beside a wood fire, telling her own fortune with an old pack of cards, spread upon a sewing board, on her capacious lap.

She was in a soiled dressing gown of purple flannel, with several of the buttons off. In the clear light of a window at the woman's back, her hair, with a groundwork of crimson, was overshot with iridescent lights. On a small table at her side a tray had been left, with the remains of *déjeuner*; a jug stained brown with streaks of coffee; a crumbled crescent roll; some balls of silver paper which had contained cream chocolates; ends of cigarettes, and a scattered grey film of ashes. At her feet a toy black Pomeranian lay coiled on the torn bodice of a red dress; and all the room was in disorder, with an indiscriminate litter of hats, gloves, French novels, feather boas, slippers, and fallen blouses or skirts.

The lady of the roses went to the mirror over the untidy mantel piece, and looked at herself, as she answered. "No luck at roulette or trente. But the best of luck outside."

"What, then?"

The girl began to hum, as she powdered her nose with a white glove, lying in a powder box.

"You remember *le beau brun?*"

"The young man in Paris you made so many enquiries about at Ritz's? Is he here?"

"He is. I've just had lunch with him. Oh, there are lots of things to tell. He is a good boy."

"How, good? You told him we had had losses?"

"I painted a sad picture. He was most sympathetic."

"To what extent?"

"*Chere maman!* One would think we were vulgar adventuresses. We are not. He respects me, this dear young man, and it is right that he should. I deserve to be respected. You know the fable about the dog who dropped his meat in the water, trying to snap at its reflection? Well, I don't ask strangers for loans. I make my impression. Monsieur Hugh Egerton is my friend—at present. Later, he will be what I choose. And most certainly I shall choose him for a husband. What luck, meeting him again! It is time I settled down."

"They said at Ritz's that he was one of the young millionaires, well known already in America," the fat woman reflected aloud. "It is a good thing that I have brought you up well, Julie, and that you are pretty."

"Yes, it is a good thing that I am pretty," repeated the girl. "We have had many hopes often before, but this seems to be the most promising. I think it is very promising indeed, and I don't mean to let it slip."

She turned her back to the easy chair, and opened the pink bag. As the woman talked on, she secretly counted out the money. There were more than ten thousand francs in mille notes and others of smaller denominations. Quietly she put them away in the top of a travelling box, which she locked.

Then she noticed the letter which the child had given her, still lying on the dressing table, with her gloves.

"Here's something from *la belle Americaine*, upstairs," said she. "A *billet doux*."

"A dun," exclaimed the woman.

"No doubt. It can be nothing else."

"Well, we can't pay."

"No, we can't pay," said the girl, looking at the locked box.

"Let me see, how much was it she lent?"

"Two hundred francs, I think. We told her we'd give it back in a week. That's nearly a month ago."

"Serve her right for trusting strangers. The saints alone know when she'll see her money again. She shouldn't be so soft hearted. It doesn't pay in these days."

"Neither do we—when we can help it."

They both laughed.

"But when you are Madame—let me see, what was the name of the young monsieur, they told you at the Ritz?"

"Egerton."

"Ah yes. When you are Madame Egerton—"

"Everything will be very different then."

And the girl slipped the key of the box into the little pink bag.

DOGS AND FATHERS

After delivering her letter, the child went slowly on downstairs, to the room she had been on the way to visit. It was on the second floor, just under the room of the Comtesse de Lavalette.

"Come in," said a Cockney voice shrill with youth, in answer to her tap; and the child obeyed.

Though this room was of the same size and shape, it was very different from that of the Comtesse. The plain furniture was stiffly arranged, and there was no litter of clothing or small feminine belongings. By the window, which gave a glimpse of the sea, and of Monaco rock with the old part of the Palace, a plump young girl sat, with a baby a year or two old in her arms, and a nurse's cap on her smooth head.

"You invited me to come down after I'd had my déjeûner, so I came," said the child.

"Right you are, Miss Rosemary," returned the plump girl. "You're such a quaint little body, you're a regular treat. I declare I ain't 'alf sure I wouldn't rather talk to you, than read the Princess Novelettes. Besides, I do get that tired of 'earin' nothin' but French, I'm most sorry I undertook the job; and the Biby don't pick up English much yet."

"Don't you think he's a bright baby?" asked the child, sitting down on a footstool, which was a favourite seat of hers.

"For a French biby, 'e 's as bright as you could expect," replied her hostess, judicially.

"Are they different?"

"Well, they ain't Hinglish."

"*I'm* half American," said the little girl.

"You don't talk through your nose. Far as I can see, you've got as good a haccent as me."

"I suppose yours *is* good?" asked Rosemary, as if she longed to have a doubt set forever at rest.

"Rather! Ain't I been brought out from London on purpose so as this biby can learn to speak Hinglish, instead of French? It's pretty near the sime thing as bein' nursery governess. Madame wouldn't trust her own wye of pronouncing the languidge. She must 'ave a Hinglish girl."

"And she sent for you on purpose?" the child enquired, with increasing respect.

"Well, I was the only one as would come at the price. 'Tain't big wages; but I'm seein' loife. Lor', I come down here with Madame and Mounseer a fortnight ago, and Monte Carlo ain't got many secrets from me. I *was* a duffer, though, at first. When I 'eerd all them shots poppin' off every few minutes, up by the Casino, I used to think 'twas the suicides a shooting theirselves all over the place, for before I left 'ome, I 'ad a warnin' from my young man that was the kind of goin's on they 'ad here. But now I know it's only the pigeon shooters, tryin' for prizes, and I wouldn't eat a pigeon pie in this 'otel, not if 'twas ever so!"

"Do they ever have them?" asked the little girl, awed.

"Not as I knows of, but they may for Christmas. I sye, are you lookin' forward to your Christmas, kiddy?"

"Angel—that's Mother, I mean—says I'm not going to have much of a Christmas this year. I'm trying not to mind. I suppose it's because Santa Claus can't get to the Riviera, with his sleigh and reindeer. How could he, Miss Jane, when there's no snow, and not even a scrap of ice?"

"Pshaw!" said Miss Jane. "It ain't Santa Claus brings you things, snow or no snow. Only babies believe that. You're old enough to know better. It's your father and mother does it all."

"Are you sure?" asked Rosemary.

"Dead sure. Don't be a silly and cry, now, just because there ain't any Santa Claus, nor any fairies."

"It isn't that," said the little girl. "It's because I can never have any more Christmases, if it depends on a father. You know, I haven't a father."

"I supposed you 'adn't, as 'e ain't 'ere, with yer ma," replied the young person. "She's mighty pretty."

"I think she's the prettiest mother in the world," said Rosemary, proudly.

"She don't look much like a mother."

The child opened her eyes very wide at this new point of view. "I couldn't have a mother who looked any other way," she said. "What do you think she does look like?"

"Silly puss! I only mean she isn't much more'n a kid, 'erself."

"She's twenty five, twenty whole years more than me. Isn't that old?"

"Lawkes, no. I'm goin' on seventeen myself. I 'avent got any father, no more'n you 'ave, so I can feel fur you. Your ma 'as to do typewritin'. Mine does charrin'. It's much the sime thing."

"Is it?" asked Rosemary. "Angel doesn't like typewriting so very well. It makes her shoulder ache, but it isn't that she minds. It's not having enough work to do."

"Bless your hinnercent 'eart, charrin' mikes you ache all *over!* Betcherlife my ma'd chinge with yours if she could."

"Would she? But Angel doesn't get on at all well here. I've heard her telling a lady she lent some money to, and wanted to have it back, after awhile. You see, when we were left poor, people said that she could make lots of money in Paris, because they pay a good deal there for the things Angel does; but others seemed to have got all the work for themselves, before we went over to Paris to live, so some friends she had told her it would be better to try here where there was no—no com—com—"

"No compertishun," suggested the would-be nursery governess.

"Yes, that's the right word, I think. But there was some, after all. Poor Angel's so sad. She doesn't quite know what we'll do next, for we haven't much money left."

"She's got a job of char—I mean, typin' to-day anyhow," said Jane.

"Yes, she's gone to a hotel, where a gentleman talks a story out loud, and she puts it down on paper. She's been three times; but it's so sad; the story is a beautiful one, only she doesn't think he'll live to finish it. He came here to get well, because there's sunshine, and flowers; but his wife cried on Angel's shoulder, in the next room to his, and said he would never, never get well any more. Angel didn't tell me, for I don't think she likes me to know sad things; but I heard her saying it all to a lady she works for sometimes, a lady who knows the poor man. I don't remember his name, but he's what they call a Genius."

"It's like that out here on the Riviera," said Jane, shaking her head so gloomily that the ruffled cap wobbled. "Lots of ill people come, as well as those who wants fun, and throwin' thur money about. In the midst of loife we are in death. Drat the Biby, I believe 'e's swallowed 'is tin soldier! No, 'ere it is, on the floor. But, as I was sayin', your ma and mine might be sisters, in some wyes. Both of 'em lost their 'usbins, young—"

"How did your father get lost?" Rosemary broke in, deeply interested.

"'E went to the dogs," replied Jane, mysteriously.

"Oh!" breathed the child, thrilled with a vague horror. She longed intensely to know what had happened to her friend's parent after joining his lot with that of the dogs, but was too delicate-minded to continue her questioning, after such a tragic beginning. She wondered if there were a kind of dreadful dog which made a specialty of eating fathers. "And did he never come back again?" she ventured to enquire, at last.

"Not 'e. You never do, you know, if once you goes to the dogs. There ain't no wye back. I was wonderin', since we've been acquainted, kiddy, if your pa didn't go the sime road? It 'appens in all clarses."

"Oh no, my father was lost at sea, not on the road; and there aren't any dogs there, at least I don't think so," said Rosemary.

"If it's only the sea 'as swallered 'im, 'e may be cast up again, any day, alive an' bloomin'," replied Jane cheerfully. "My ma 'ad a grite friend, sold winkles; 'er 'usbin was lost at sea for years and years, till just wen she was comfortably settled with 'er second, along 'e comes, as large as loife. Besides, I've read of such things in the Princess Novelettes; only there it's most generally lovers, not 'usbins, nor yet fathers. Would you know yours again, if you seen 'im?"

Rosemary shook her head doubtfully, and her falling hair of pale, shimmering gold waved like a wheat-field shaken by a breeze. "Angel lost him when I was only two," the child explained. "She's never talked much to me about him; but we used to live in a big house in London—because my father was English, you know, though Angel's American—and I had a nurse who held me in her lap and told me things. I heard her say to one of the servants once that my father had been lost on a yacht, and that he was oh, ever such a handsome man. But—but she said—" Rosemary faltered, her grey-blue eyes suddenly large and troubled.

"What was it she said?" prompted Jane, with so much sympathetic interest that the little girl could not refuse to answer. Nevertheless, she felt that it would not be right to finish her sentence.

"If you please, I'd rather not tell you what Nurse said," she pleaded. "But anyway, I'd give everything I've got if my father would get found again. You see, it isn't only not having proper Christmases any more, that makes me feel sad, it's because Angel has to work so hard for me; and if I had a father, I s'pose he'd do that."

"If 'e didn't he'd deserve to get What For," said Jane, decidedly. "If you was a child in a story book, your pa'd come back and be lookin' for you everywhere, on Christmas Eve; this Christmas Eve as ever was."

"Oh, would he?" cried Rosemary, a bright colour flaming on her little soft cheeks.

"Yes; and what's more," went on her hostess, warming to the subject, "you'd know 'im, the hinstant you clapped heyes on his fice, by 'eaven-sent hinstinct."

"What's 'eaven-sent hinstinct?" demanded Rosemary.

"The feelin' you 'ave in your 'eart for a father, wot's planted there by Providence," explained Jane. "Now do you hunderstand? Because if you do, I don't know but you'd better be trottin'. Biby's gorn to sleep, and seems to be sleepin' light."

"Yes, I think I understand," Rosemary whispered, jumping up from her footstool. "Goodbye. And thank you very much for letting me come and see you and the baby."

She tiptoed across the room, her long hair waving and shimmering again, softly opened, and shut the door behind her, and slowly mounted the stairs to her own quarters, on the fourth floor.

ROSEMARY IN SEARCH OF A FATHER

She had a doll and a picture book there, but she had looked at the picture book hundreds of times; and though her doll was a faithful friend, somehow they had nothing to say to each other now. Rosemary flitted about like a will o' the wisp, and finally went to the window, where she stood looking wistfully out.

Supposing that Jane were right, and her father came back out of the ocean like the fathers of little girls in story books, this might be a very likely place for him to land, because there was such lots of sea, beautiful, sparkling, blue sea. Of course, he couldn't know that Angel and she were in this town, because it was only about a month since they came. It must be difficult to hear things in ships; and he might go away, to look for them somewhere else, without ever finding them here.

Little thrills of excitement running from Rosemary's fingers to her toes felt like vibrating wires. What could she do? Jane had said, if he came at all, he was sure to come on Christmas Eve, according to the habit of fathers, and it was Christmas Eve now. By and bye it would be too late, anyhow for a whole year, which was just the same as forever and ever. Oh, she must go out, this very minute!

The child had put on her hat and coat, before she remembered that Angel had told her she must never stir beyond the hotel garden alone. But then, Angel probably did not know this important fact about fathers lost at sea, returning on Christmas Eve, and not at any other time.

If she waited until Angel came in, it might be after sunset, as it had been yesterday; and then even if they hurried into the street to search, they could not recognize him in the dark.

"I do think Angel would surely want me to go, if she knew," thought Rosemary.

Her heart was beating fast, under the little dark blue coat. What a glorious surprise for Angel, if she could bring a tall, handsome man into this room, and say, "Dearest, now you won't have to work any more, or cry in the night when you think I've gone to sleep. Here's father, come back out of the sea."

"Oh, oh!" she cried, and ran from the room, afraid of wasting another instant.

The sallow young concierge had often seen the child go out alone to disappear round the path that circled the hotel, and play in the dusty square of grass which, on the strength of two orange trees and a palm, was called a garden. He thought nothing of it now, when she nodded in her polite little way, and opened the door for herself. Five minutes later, he was reading of a delicious jewel robbery, which had happened in a tunnel near Nice, and had forgotten all about Rosemary's existence.

The little girl had an idea that she ought to go to the place where ships came in, and as she had more than once walked to the port with her mother, she knew the way very well.

Two white yachts were riding at anchor in the harbour, but no one had come on shore who looked handsome enough for a father to be recognised by 'eaven-sent-hinstinct, the moment you set eyes upon him. Rosemary stood by the quay for a few minutes, uncertain what to do. Two or three deep-eyed, long-lashed Monegasque men smiled at her kindly, as Monegasque men and Italians smile at all children. She had learned to lisp French with comparative fluency, during the months she and "Angel" had spent in Paris; and now she asked where the people went who had come in on those pretty white ships?

"Those are yachts," said one of the deep-eyed men; "and the people who come on them are rowed to shore in little boats. Then they go quickly up the hill, to the Casino—that big white building there—so that they can put their money on a table, or take somebody else's money off."

"I have always seen dishes put on tables," said Rosemary, "never money. If I went there, could I take some off? I should like to have a little, very much."

"So would we all," smiled the deep-eyed man, patting her head. "They would not let you in, because you are too young."

"I want to find my father, who has been on the sea," the child explained. "Do you think he might be there?"

"He is sure to be there," said the deep-eyed man; and he and the other men laughed. "If you sit on a bench where the grass and flowers are, outside the Casino door, and watch, perhaps you will see him come down the steps. But you are small to be out all alone looking for him."

"It's very important for me to find my father before it is dark," said Rosemary. "So I thank you for telling me, and now goodbye."

Daintily polite as usual, she bowed to them all, and started up the hill.

As she walked briskly on, she studied with large, starry eyes the face of every man she met; but there was not a suitable father among them. She was still fatherless when she reached the Place of the Casino, where she had often come before, to walk in the gardens or on the terrace at unfashionable hours with her mother, on Sundays, or other days when—unfortunately—there was no work to do.

She had sat down on a bench between a French "nou-nou," with a wonderful head dress, and a hawk-visaged old lady with a golden wig, and had fixed her eyes upon the Casino door, when the throb, throb of a motor caught her attention.

Now an automobile was a marvellous dragon for Rosemary, and she could never see too many for her pleasure. Above all things, she would have loved a spin on the back of such a dragon, and she liked choosing favourites from among the dragon brood.

A splendid dark blue one was panting and quivering before the door of the Hotel de Paris, having just been started by a slim chauffeur in a short fur coat. As Rosemary gazed, deciding that this was the noblest dragon of them all, a young man ran down the steps of the hotel and got into the car. He took his place in the driver's seat, laid his hand on the steering wheel as if he were caressing a baby's head, the chauffeur sprang up beside his master, and they were off. But with a cry, Rosemary rushed across the road.

The nou-nou shrieked and hugged her muffled charge; the old lady screamed, and all the other old ladies and young ladies, and pretty girls sitting on the benches, or walking about, screamed too.

The man who drove was pale under his coat of brown tan as with a crash of machinery he brought the big blue car to a stop so close to the child that its glittering bonnet touched her coat. He did not say a word for an instant, for his lips were pressed so tightly together, that they were a white line.

With a crash of machinery he brought the big blue car to a stop.

—*Rosemary.*

That beautiful, little golden-haired, smiling thing, so full of life! But it was all right now. She was smiling still, as if she did not guess the deadly peril she had just escaped.

"Don't you know, little one," he asked gently, "that it's very dangerous to run in front of automobiles?"

"Oh, but I wanted so much to stop you," said Rosemary.

"Why, do you know me?" And the young man smiled such a pleasant smile, with a gleam of white teeth, that the child was more than ever sure she had done right.

"Yes, I know you by 'eavensenthinstinct." She got out the long word with a gasp or two; but it was a great success. She had not mixed up a single syllable.

The young man burst out laughing. "Where's your nurse?" he asked.

"In London," said Rosemary. "She isn't my nurse any more."

"Well, your mother—"

"She isn't—"

"What? Are you going to tell me she isn't your mother any more? Are you out 'on your own,' little lady?"

"I don't know what that is; and my mother's my mother just as usual, thank you," said Rosemary, with dignity. "She's quite well. But she doesn't know I came out to look for you."

"Oh, doesn't she?" echoed the young man in the car. "Then don't you think the best thing you can do is to let me take you back to her?"

"She won't be home yet, not till it's dark, I expect," said the child.

"Oh, that's a long time yet. Well, since you know me, wouldn't you like to climb in, and have a little run?"

"May I, truly and really?" The little face grew pink with joy.

"Truly and really—if you're not afraid."

"What should I be afraid of?" Rosemary asked.

"I was talking nonsense. Get down, Paul, and put her into the tonneau. You'd better sit by her, perhaps."

The chauffeur proceeded to obey, but when the child found herself being tucked into a back seat of the car, she gave a little protesting cry. "Oh, can't I sit in front with you?"

"Of course you can, if you like. Paul, wrap her up well in the rug. Now, little one, we're going to start. I won't take you too fast."

He turned the car, and passing the Casino drove up the hill, taking the direction of Mentone, when he had reached the top. He had not been over this road before, as he had arrived by way of Nice yesterday; but he had studied road maps, and knew both how and where he wished to go.

"Now," said he, driving carefully, "how do you like it?"

"Oh, it's wonderful!" answered Rosemary, with a rapt smile on her rosy face.

"Have you ever motored before?"

She shook her head. "Never."

"Brave Baby."

"I don't usually care to be called a baby," she remarked. "But I don't mind from you."

"I'm especially favoured, it seems," said the young man. "Tell me how you happen to know me? I can't think, I must confess, unless it was on shipboard—"

"There! I knew perfectly well it was you!" broke in Rosemary with a look of rapture. "You *were* on a ship, and you were lost at sea. But you're found again now, because it's Christmas Eve."

"I wasn't lost at sea, though, or I shouldn't be here with you," said Hugh Egerton. He glanced rather wistfully in a puzzled way at the lovely little face framed with blowing golden hair. There was something in the child's eyes which stabbed his heart; yet there was sweetness in the pain. "I'm afraid we're playing at cross purposes, aren't we?" he went on. "Was it on a ship that you saw me?"

"Oh, I didn't see you on the ship," said Rosemary. "I only knew you went away on one. I haven't seen you for ever and ever so long, not since I was a tiny baby."

"By Jove! And you've remembered me all this time?"

"Not exactly remembered. It was the feeling I had in my heart, just as Jane said I would, the minute I saw you, that told me it was you. That was why I ran to keep you from going on in your motor car, because if you had, I might have lost you again, forever and ever."

"So you might," said puzzled Hugh Egerton, pleased as well as puzzled. "And that would never have done for either of us."

"It would have been dreadful," replied Rosemary, "to have to wait for another Christmas Eve."

"Christmas Eve seems a day for adventures," said Hugh. "One finds new friends;—and dear little girls; and—goodness knows what I shall find next."

"We must find Angel next," Rosemary assured him. "She'll be so glad to see you."

"Do you really think so? By the way, who is Angel?"

"Mother. Didn't you know *that?*"

"I expect I'd forgotten," Hugh answered. She looked so reproachful, that not for the world would he have denied all knowledge of Angel. The child evidently took him for someone she had known; perhaps she had seen a photograph of some long lost friend of her family, who resembled him, and she had sprung to a conclusion, as children do. But she was an exquisitely pretty and engaging little thing, a grand little pal, and worth cultivating. Hugh liked children, especially girls, though he had always been rather shy with them, not knowing exactly how they liked best to be entertained, and finding it difficult to think of things to say, in keeping up a conversation. But there was no such difficulty with this child. It was really interesting to draw the little creature out, and see what she would say next. As for finding Angel, however, when the time came to do that, he thought he would prefer to bid Angel's daughter goodbye at the door. He had no fancy for scraping up an acquaintance with strangers through their children.

FAIRY FATHERS MUST VANISH

Rosemary sat in silence for a few moments, taking in the full meaning of her companion's answer to her last question. He had forgotten that Angel was Angel! Though she was warmly wrapped in a soft rug of silvery fur, a chill crept into her heart. Could it be that Nurse's words about father had been true, after all; and if they were, was she doing harm, rather than good, in bringing him home?

Presently Hugh waked out of his own thoughts, and noticed the little girl's silence.

"You're not afraid?" he asked, blissfully unconscious of offence. "I'm not driving too fast to please you?"

"Oh no," said Rosemary.

"You're not cold?"

"No, thank you."

"Nor tired?"

"No, not tired."

"But something is the matter?"

"I'm worrying," confessed the child.

"What about, little one?"

"I'm not sure if I ought to have spoken to you, or have come with you, after all."

To save his life, Hugh could not have helped laughing, though it was evidently a matter of serious importance. "What, do you think we ought to have a chaperon?" he asked. "Paul's in the tonneau, you know; and he's a most discreet chap."

"I don't know what a chaperon is," said Rosemary. "But will you promise not to be angry if I ask you something, and will you promise to answer, honour bright?"

"Yes, to both your questions."

"Were you really unkind to Angel, before you were lost?"

This was a hard nut to crack, if his past were not to be ruthlessly severed from Angel's by a word. He thought for a moment, and then said, "Honour bright, I can't remember anything unkind I ever did to her."

"Oh, I'm so glad. I was afraid, when you said you'd forgotten—but maybe her name wasn't Angel, then?"

"That was it, I'm sure," replied Hugh, soothingly. "Maybe you named her Angel, yourself?"

"I don't know," said Rosemary. "She seems to have been it, always, ever since I can remember. And she does look just like one, you know, she's so beautiful."

"I expect you remember a lot more about angels than I do, because it isn't so long since you came from where they live. But here we are in the woods at Cap Martin. Have you ever been here before?"

"Angel and I had a picnic here once, all by ourselves; and there were lots of sheep under the olive trees, and a funny old shepherd who made music to them. Oh, I do love picnics, don't you? Angel said, if she were rich, she'd take me on the loveliest kind of a picnic for Christmas; but, you see, it would cost too much money to do it, for we've hardly got any, especially since the Comtesse doesn't pay us back."

"What kind of picnic would it have been?" asked Hugh, driving along the beautiful shore road, where the wind-blown pines lean forward like transformed wood nymphs, caught in a spell just as they spread out their arms to spring into the sea.

"Angel has told me lots of history-stories about the strange rock-villages in the mountains. There's one called Éze, on top of a hill shaped almost like a horn; she showed me a picture of it. Children live up in the rock villages, and never come down to the towns. They've never even seen any toys, like other children play with, Angel says. All the strangers who come here give presents to the poor in Monte Carlo and Mentone, and big places like that; but they never think of the ones up in the mountains. Angel said how nice it would be, if we were rich, to buy toys,—baskets and baskets full,—and give them away to the children of Éze. Perhaps you are rich; are you?"

"Richer than I thought, a few years ago, that I ever should be. I used to be poor, until I dug, and found some gold lying about in the ground."

"How splendid! I suppose the fairies showed you where to look. Jane says there are no fairies, but I do hope she's mistaken. I wish you would send up some presents to the little children at Éze."

"I will, lots, if you'll take them."

"Perhaps we could all go together."

"I'm afraid your mother wouldn't care for that."

"Yes, she would. Because, if you were never unkind to her, like Nurse said you were, she'll be most awfully glad to see you again. I shouldn't wonder if she'd cry for joy, to have you with us always, and take care of us. Oh, do let's go back now, and I'll take you to her. She *will* be surprised!"

"I should think she would," said Hugh. "But look here; you said she wouldn't get back till dark. We've come to Mentone now. See how pretty the shops are for Christmas. Can't you stop and have some nice hot chocolate and cakes with me, and afterwards choose a doll for yourself, as a Christmas present from your old friend?"

As he put this temptation before her, he slowed down the car in front of a shop with big glass windows full of sparkling cakes, and ribbon-tied baskets of crystallized fruits. Through the windows Rosemary could see a great many well-dressed people sitting at little marble tables, and it would have been delightful to go in. But she shook her head. The sun was setting over the sea. The sky was flooded with pink and gold, while all the air was rosy with a wonderful glow which painted the mountains, even the dappled-grey plane trees, and the fronts of the gaily decorated shops.

The donkey women were leading their patient little animals away from the stand on the sea promenade, up to Sorbio for the night; and their dark faces under the queer, mushroom hats were ruddy and beautiful in the rose-light.

"As soon as the sun goes down, it gets dark here," said Rosemary, regretfully. "Thank you very much, but I'd rather go home now. You see, I do *so* want you to be there already, waiting to surprise Angel when she comes in."

"No time even to buy a doll?"

"I'd rather go home, thank you. Besides, though I should like to have a new doll, perhaps darling Evie would be sad if I played with another."

Hugh was obediently turning the car's bonnet towards Monte Carlo, and for the fraction of a second he was foolish enough almost to lose control of it, on account of a start he gave. "Evie!" he echoed.

It was years since he had spoken that name.

"She's my doll," explained Rosemary.

"Oh!" said Hugh.

"But I don't think she'd mind or be sad if you gave me a doll's house," went on the child, "if you *should* have time to get it for me by and bye; that is, if you really want to give me something for Christmas, you know."

"Of course I do. But tell me, why did you name your doll Evie?"

He put the question in a low voice, as if he were half ashamed of asking it; and as at that instant a tram boomed by, Rosemary heard only the first words.

"I 'sposed you would," she replied. "Fathers do like to give their little girls Christmas presents, Jane says; maybe that's why they're obliged to come back always on Christmas Eve, if they've been lost. Do you know, even if there aren't any fairies, it's just like a fairy story having my father come back, and take me to Angel in a motor car on Christmas eve."

"Good gracious!" exclaimed Hugh Egerton. "Did you say—father?"

"Yes," replied Rosemary. "You're almost like a fairy father, I said."

So, he was her father—her long lost father! Poor little lamb, he began to guess at the story now. There was a scamp of a father who had "not been very kind" to Angel, and had been lost, or had thoughtfully lost himself. For some extraordinary reason the child imagined that he—well, if it were not pathetic, it would be funny. But somehow he did not feel much inclined to laugh. Poor little thing! His heart yearned over her; but the situation was becoming strained. Unless he could think of some good way out of it, he might have a scene when he was obliged to rob the child of her father, on reaching the door of her house.

"That's it," said he, calling all his tact to the rescue. "I am a fairy father. Just as you thought, it's a mistake of Jane's about there being no fairies; only the trouble is, fairies aren't so powerful as they used to be in the old days. Now, I should love to be able to stay with you for a long, long time, but because I'm only a poor fairy father, I can't. We've been very happy together, and I'm tremendously glad you found me. I shall think of you and of this day, often. But the cruel part is, that when I bring you to your door, I'm afraid I shall have to—vanish."

"Oh, how dreadful!" cried Rosemary, her voice quivering. "Must I lose you again?"

"Perhaps I can write to you," Hugh tried to console her, feeling horribly guilty and helpless.

"That won't be the same. I do love you so much. *Please* don't vanish."

"I shall send you things. A doll's house for Evie. By the way, you didn't tell me why you named her that."

"After Angel, of course," returned the child absent-mindedly. "But when you've vanished, I—"

"Is your mother's name Evie?"

"Evelyn. But that's too long for a doll."

"Evelyn—what? You—you haven't told me your name yet."

"Rosemary Evelyn Clifford."

"Great Heavens!"

"How strange your voice sounds," said Rosemary. "Are you ill?"

"No—no! I—feel a little odd, that's all."

"Oh, it isn't the vanishing coming on already? We're a long way from our hotel yet."

Hugh drove mechanically, though sky and sea and mountains seemed to be seething together, as if in the convulsions of an earthquake.

Her child! And her husband—what of him? The little one said he was lost; that he had not been kind. Hugh gritted his teeth together, and heard only the singing of his blood in his ears. Was the man dead, or had he but disappeared? In any case, *she* was here, alone in Monte Carlo, with her child; poor, unhappy, working by day, crying by night. He must see her, at once—at once.

Yet—what if it were not she, after all? If the name were a coincidence? There might be other Evelyn Cliffords in the world. It must be that this was another. His Evelyn had married a rich and titled Englishman. She was Lady Clifford. The things that had happened to Rosemary's Angel could not have happened to her. Still, he must know, and know quickly.

"Where do you live, little Rosemary?" he asked, grimly schooling his voice, when he felt that he could trust himself to speak.

"The Hotel Pensior Beau Soleil, Rue Girasole, in the Condamine, Monte Carlo," answered the child, as if she were repeating a lesson she had been taught to rattle off by heart.

Lost as he was to most external things, Hugh roused himself to some surprise at the name of the hotel.

"Why, that is where Mademoiselle de Lavalette and her mother live!" he exclaimed.

"They're the ladies Angel lent the money to, because she was so sorry for them," said Rosemary. "I've heard them talking about it with her, and saying they can't pay it back. They're angry with her for asking, but she had to, you see. When they go past us in the dining-room they turn their backs."

Hugh's attention was arrested now.

"Do they dine?" he asked. "Every night?"

"Oh yes, always. Mademoiselle has lovely dresses. She is pretty, but the Comtesse is such an ugly old lady; like Red Riding Hood's grandmother, I think. I'm afraid of her. Jane says *her* Madame and Monsieur don't believe she's really a Comtesse. I had to knock at her door with a letter from Angel to-day, for Angel doesn't know I'm afraid. I couldn't help being glad Madame wouldn't let me in, for it seemed as if she might eat me up. I knocked and knocked, and when I was going away, I saw Mademoiselle coming in, in a pink dress with a rosy hat."

"I think she'll pay your mother back to-morrow," said Hugh, remembering the fatness of the pink bag.

"She didn't say she would. She was so cross with me that she called me a *petit bête*, and snatched the letter out of my hand."

At this, Hugh's face grew suddenly hot and red, and he muttered something under his breath. But it was not a word which Rosemary would have understood, even if she had heard.

THE WHITE FIGURE AT THE DOOR

Rosemary had tears in her eyes and voice, when the fairy father stopped his car at the door of the hotel. He had driven so very quickly since he'd broken it to her that they must part!

"Now, have you to vanish this very minute?" she asked, choking back a sob, as he lifted her to the ground.

Vanish? He had forgotten all about vanishing. To vanish now was the last thing he wished to do.

"Something tells me that I shan't have to,—quite yet, anyhow," he said hastily. "I—want to see your mother. Has she a sitting-room where I could call upon her, or wait till she comes in?"

"We haven't one of our own," said Rosemary. "But there's a nice old lady who lives next door to us, on the top floor, and is very good to Angel and me. She writes stories, and things for the papers, and Angel types them, sometimes. When she's away she lets us use the sitting-room where she writes; and she's away now. Angel and I are going to be there this evening till it's my bed-time; and you can come up with me if you will. Oh, I'm so thankful you don't need to vanish for a little while."

His heart pounding as it had not pounded for six years and more—(not since the days when he had gone up other stairs, in another land, to see an Evelyn)—Hugh followed the flitting figure of the child.

The stairs and corridors were not lighted yet. One economises with electric light and many other little things at a hotel pension, where the prices are "from five francs a day, *vin compris*."

Rosemary opened a door on the fourth floor, and for a moment the twilight on the other side was shot for Hugh with red and purple spots. But the colours faded when the childish voice said, "Angel isn't here. If you'll come in, I'll go and see if she's in our room."

"Don't tell her—don't say—anything about a fairy father," he stammered.

"Oh no, that's to be the surprise," Rosemary reassured him, as she pattered away.

It was deep twilight in the room, and rather cold, for the eucalyptus and olive logs in the fireplace still awaited the match. Hugh could see the blurred outlines of a few pieces of cheap furniture; a sofa, three or four chairs, a table, and a clumsy writing desk. But the window was still a square of pale bluish light, cut out of the violet dusk, and as the young man's eyes accustomed themselves to the dimness, the room did not seem dark.

He was not left alone for long. In two or three minutes Rosemary appeared once more, without her hat and coat, to say that "Angel" had not yet come back. "But she'll soon be here now," went on the child. "Do you mind waiting in the twilight, fairy father? The electric light doesn't come on till after five, and I've just heard the clock downstairs strike five."

"I shall like it," answered Hugh, glad that his face should be hidden by the dusk, in these moments of waiting.

"Angel tells me stories in the twilight," said Rosemary, as he sat down on the sofa by the cold fireplace, and she let him lift her light little body to his knee. "Would you tell me one, about when you were lost?"

"I'll try," Hugh said. "Let me think, what story shall I tell?"

"I won't speak while you're remembering," Rosemary promised, leaning her head confidingly against his shoulder. "I always keep quiet, while Angel puts on her thinking cap."

Hugh laughed, and was silent. But his head was too hot to wear a thinking cap, and no story would come at his half-hearted call.

Rosemary waited in patience for him to begin. "One, two, three," she counted under her breath; for she had learned to count up to fifty, and it was good practice when one wished to make the time pass. She had just come to forty-nine, and was wondering if she might remind the fairy father of his duty, when the door opened.

It was Angel, of course; but Angel did not come in. She stopped on the threshold, talking to somebody, or rather somebody was talking to her. Rosemary could not see the person, but she recognised the voice. It was that of Mademoiselle de Lavalette.

"You are not to write my mother letters, and trouble us about that money, madame," said the voice, as shrill now as it could be sweet. "Once for all, I will not have it. I have followed you to tell you this. You will be paid soon; that is enough. I am engaged to be married to a rich man, an American. He will be glad to pay all our debts by and by; but meantime, madame, you are to let us alone."

"I have done nothing, except to write and say that I needed the money,— which you promised to return weeks ago, or I couldn't possibly have spared it," protested a voice which Hugh had heard in dreams three nights out of every six, in as many years.

"Well, if you write any more letters, we shall burn them unread, so it is no use to trouble us; and we will pay when we choose."

With the last words, the other voice died into distance. Mademoiselle had said what she came to say, and was retreating with dignity down the corridor.

Now the figure of a slender woman was silhouetted in the doorway. Hugh heard a sigh, and saw a hand that glimmered white in the dusk against the dark paper on the wall, as it groped for the button of the electric light. Then, suddenly the room was filled with a white radiance, and she stood in the midst of it, young and beautiful, the woman he had loved for seven years.

Putting Rosemary away he sprang up, and her eyes, dazzled at first by the sudden flood of light, opened wide in startled recognition. "Hugh—Hugh Egerton!" she stammered, whispering as one whispers in a dream.

She was pale as a lily, but the whiteness of her face was like light, shining from within; and there was a light in her great eyes, too, such as had never shone for Hugh on sea or land. Once, a long time ago, he had hoped that she cared, or would come to care. But she had chosen another man, and Hugh had gone away; that had been the end. Yet now—what stars her eyes were! One might almost think that she had not forgotten; that sometimes she had wished for him, that she was glad to see him now.

"Lady Clifford," he stammered. "I—will you forgive my being here—my frightening you like this?"

The brightness died out of her face. "Lady Clifford!" she echoed. "Don't call me that, unless—I'm to call you Mr. Egerton? And besides, I'm only Madame Clifford here. It is better; the other would seem like ostentation in a woman who works."

"Evelyn," he said. "Thank you for letting it be Evelyn." Then, his voice breaking a little, "Oh, say you're a tiny bit glad to see me, just a tiny bit glad."

She did not answer in words; but her eyes spoke, as she held out both hands.

He crushed them in his, then bent his head and kissed them.

—Rosemary.

He crushed them in his, then bent his head and kissed them; first the girlish right hand, then the left. But she saw his face contract as he caught the gleam of her wedding ring. As he looked up, their eyes met again, and each knew what was in the other's mind.

"Angel, dearest," said Rosemary, "do tell the fairy father you're glad to see him."

Evelyn started. "Why do you call him that?"

"Because he said he was a fairy, and would have to vanish soon. But you'll beg him not to, won't you?"

"I—I should be sorry to lose him again. We haven't many friends, in these days." The bright head was bowed over the child's, as Rosemary clung to her mother's dress.

"You never lost me," said Hugh Egerton. "It was I who lost you. Evie, you don't know what black years these have been. I loved you so."

"But that—was—long ago."

"It was always."

"Hugh! I thought you must have learned to hate me."

"Hate you, because I couldn't make you care for me as—I hoped you would, and because you cared for someone else? No, I—"

"But—I did care for you. It was for my father's sake that—that—ah, I can't talk of it, Hugh. You know, we were so poor after father lost his money, I tried with all my heart to forget, and to do my best for—my husband. Perhaps it was my punishment that he—oh, Hugh, I was so miserable. And then—then he went away. He was tired of me. He was on a yacht, and there was a great storm. But you must have read in the papers—"

"Never. I never knew till this day."

"It was more than three years ago."

Hugh was very pale. Three years ago—three long years in which he had worked, and tried not to think of her! And if he had known—"You see, I've had a queer life, knocking about in strange places," he said, trying to speak calmly. "Often I didn't see any newspapers for weeks together. I thought of you always as rich and happy, living in England, the wife of Sir Edward Clifford—"

"Rich and happy," she repeated, bitterly. "How little one knows of another's life. After his death, there was nothing—there had been some wild speculations; and the estates went with the title, of course, to his cousin. But, yes,—in a way you were right. I was rich and happy because I had Rosemary."

"And Rosemary had you, Angel," cried the child, who had been listening, puzzled and bewildered, not knowing that they had forgotten her presence until this moment. "Rosemary had you. And now we've all got each other— till the fairy father vanishes."

"But I shan't have to vanish after all," said Hugh.

After that, it seemed they had been together but for a moment, when a wild wail went moaning through the house; the first gong for the *pensionnaires'* dinner.

So loud it was that it hushed their voices for a long minute. And when cool silence came again, Hugh begged that the two would have their Christmas

Eve dinner with him, at his hotel. "There's so much to plan for to-morrow, and all the days," he pleaded. "And just for once Rosemary shall have a late dinner like the grown-ups. Do say yes."

So Evelyn said yes. And it was not until they were all three seated in the restaurant of the Hotel de Paris, that he remembered he had been engaged to dine at the Beau Soleil with Mademoiselle and the Comtesse, her mother.

But he did not even blush because he had forgotten.

WHEN A MAN GOES SHOPPING

Many of Hugh Egerton's best moments during the last six years had been spent in dreams. In those dreams the past had lived again; for he had seen the future as once he had hoped it might be for him.

But all through this night of Christmas Eve he lay awake; and no dreams had ever been as half as sweet as the thoughts that came to him then. It would have been a hideous waste of time to sleep, when he could lie there and live over again each moment of his evening, beginning at the beginning, when She had come into the room, and going on to the end when he had brought her and Rosemary to the door of the Hotel Pension Beau Soleil, to say "goodbye until to-morrow." When he came to the end, he went back to the beginning again with renewed zest, trying to call up some word, some look of hers which he might have neglected to count among his treasured jewels.

Then, when he was sure that he had each pearl and ruby and diamond duly polished and strung on the fine gold chain of loving memory, he would let his mind run ahead of time, to the next day.

What a Christmas it was going to be! There never had been one like it before, in the history of the world; but—the best of it was—there was reason to hope that there would be many others to come just as exquisite, if not more perfect.

Evelyn Clifford had loved him, even when she had let him go. She loved him now; and she had promised to make up for the long grey years of the past by marrying him almost at once.

There was nothing to wait for. He was lonely and rich. She was lonely and poor. Both were young, and starving for happiness. In a week they would be married, for she had promised to begin the New Year as his wife. Meanwhile, there would be a great deal to do (so she said, though he could not see why) in getting ready. But Christmas was to be a holiday. They were going on that picnic to Éze, all three. That was already planned; but Hugh had mentally made an addition to the plan, of which he had said not a word.

He was as excited over the thought of this plan as Rosemary would have been had she known. And lest there should be a hitch, or he should not have time to accomplish all, he was out of bed by half past six—that mysterious hour of dawn when across the glimmering sea Corsica can be seen, floating like a heaped basket of violets in waves of transparent gold.

Last night he had anxiously enquired of the concierge whether the Monte Carlo shops would be open on Christmas morning, and had been informed that they would. Otherwise, Hugh Egerton would have been capable of battering down the doors, helping himself to the things he wanted, and leaving enough money to pay for damages as well as purchases.

After all, he was ready long before the shutters of those attractive plate glass windows were taken away; but he was not sorry for that. He had the joy of walking down to the Condamine and gazing up at other windows far more attractive, and saying to the closed green blinds, "Merry Christmas, merry Christmas, my darling—mine for always, now!"

Then he darted back to rolls and coffee; beamed on the waiters, gave them fat five franc pieces merely for beaming in return; and arrived in the Galerie Charles Trois just as the shop windows were opening radiant Christmas eyes.

The first visit he paid was to the florist's; and to save time in choosing he simply said, "I'll take all those things you have in the window, please."

There were about two hundred francs worth of roses, the same of white lilacs, and enough lilies of the valley, nestling in baby leaves of yellow green, to clean out any save a well-filled pocket book; but that was all the better. The more he could spend to-day, the more was Hugh Egerton pleased. He gave "Madame Clifford's" address, and wrote something in English on his visiting card. The flowers were to go at once; at once, mind; not in fifteen minutes, but now, this very now.

"How much in love is that handsome young Monsieur!" thought the Mademoiselle of the shop, with a little sigh for some of the wonders of the world which she had missed, and must always miss. Her heels were appallingly high, and her waist was incredibly small; but she had a heart; and there was no heart which would not have softened to Hugh, and wished him the best of good luck, this day.

The next window which attracted the young man's eye, was one which displayed just such a dress as he had vaguely pictured yesterday, for a dear companion on the terrace. It was white, of course; and he was not sure, but he thought it was made of cloth. Anyway there was a lot of embroidery on it, full of little holes, which somehow contrived to be extraordinarily fetching. It had a mantle which hung in soft folds, marvellously intricate, yet simple in effect; and he could have fallen upon the neck of the stout, powdered lady in black silk who assured him that the costume could be worn without alteration by any "*dame de jolie taille.*"

He bought it instantly, and then seized upon precisely such a "long white thing" of ermine as he had seen in his mind's eye. A "granny" muff went with it. (Really the people of the shop must have had prophetic souls!) And there was a white hat, with a gold buckle and a long white ostrich feather which looked as if it had been born to shade the face of Evelyn Clifford.

When these "confections" had been secured, Madame of the black satin and powdered nose assured Monsieur that his Christmas purchases would be incomplete without a certain blouse which, to an untutored eye, appeared to be a combination of sea-foam and rose-leaves. There was a belt, too, crusted with seed pearls; and a hanging bag to match. Oh, certainly Monsieur would take these, and anything else which Madame could conscientiously recommend. She could, and did, recommend several other things; and no doubt it was a mere coincidence that they happened to be among the most expensive in the shop. She also won Hugh's gratitude by being able to produce a coat and a frock in which a little girl of five, already beautiful, would be more akin to fairyhood than ordinary childhood, and might become the "exception that would prove the rule" to an unbelieving Jane.

The cloak was pale blue; and another shop had to be searched for a hat to be worn with it, but Madame was most kind in directing Monsieur where to find one. Her sister would serve him, therefore he would be well served.

On the way, he passed a jeweller's; and exactly the right string of pearls, and the right "swallow brooch" stared him in the face, in the window. It was odd, how all the prettiest things in the world, of whatever description, looked as if they ought to belong to Evelyn and Rosemary Clifford. There was a gold bag, too; but that was a detail, for really the principal thing he had called for was a ring with a single diamond in it—and perhaps—well, yes—that little sapphire band to keep it on a slender finger.

The rings, in their delicate cases, he put into his pocket when he had paid; but the other purchases were to go in that very same now which had been impressed upon the florist; the sort of now to which Riviera shopkeepers are accustomed only when they deal with Americans.

Then Madame's sister was found, and a blue hat; and there was just time left for a frantic rush to a toyshop, round a corner and up a hill. Perhaps Doll Evie might be jealous of one rival, but there's safety in numbers; and Hugh thought that a dozen assorted sizes, from life-size down, would keep a doll's house from echoing with loneliness. As for the presents for the Éze children, Rosemary was to choose them herself by and by; but all these special things were to be served up, so to speak, at the Hotel Pension Beau Soleil with early breakfast.

When he had finished,—which means, when he had bought everything he could think of—Hugh looked at his watch. It was half an hour to the minute since he had left his hotel.

"I don't see why it should take women a long time to shop," said he to himself. "It seems to me the simplest thing in the world. You just see what you want, and then you buy it."

It was not until all the boxes and parcels must have arrived in the Condamine, that an agonizing thought struck Hugh. What if Evie should be offended with him for buying her things to wear? What if she should imagine him capable of thinking that the things she already had were not good enough when she was coming out with him?

He suddenly felt a hundred years old. "Ass—worm—menagerie!" he anathematized himself.

It was now nine thirty. At ten forty-five he was to call at the Hotel Pension Beau Soleil, to take Evelyn and Rosemary to the English church. How could he bear the suspense till then,—how endure it not to know whether he had ruined the Christmas which was to have been so perfect?

He dashed into his own hotel, wrote five notes one after the other, tearing up each one before it was finished. It was no good explaining. If she didn't understand nothing would make her. But *would* she understand? He knew now why some women said that all men were fools. They were quite right.

If he had dared, he would have gone to her at once, to be put out of his misery, one way or the other. But he did not dare; so he waited, until he had persuaded himself that not only his watch, but the hotel clock and the Casino clock must be slow.

Then he started, and suffered five suffocating minutes in the public sitting-room of the Beau Soleil. It was a hideous room, with abominable flowers sprawling over the wall paper and carpet, and all the windows were shut, but he did not notice these things; nor did he recognise the heavy scent that hung in the air as that which Mademoiselle de Lavalette affected. The lady of the roses had ceased to exist for him; but, if he had thought of her at all, he would have been glad that he had opened her pink leather bag when it was thin, and shut it up when it was very fat.

At the end of the five minutes, the door opened, and gave to his eyes a vision; Evelyn and Rosemary in their new dresses and new hats.

It was all he could do to keep from crying "Thank Heaven," and to say a mere "Merry Christmas" instead.

"Wicked, extravagant Boy," exclaimed Evelyn. "Do you know, we are most unsuitably dressed? But we *had* to put the things on, hadn't we? It was wrong of you to buy them, but—don't look so terrified—it was sweet, too; and I know just the feeling that prompted you to do it. What a dream-Christmas this is going to be."

And then she and Rosemary thanked him separately, for each individual thing he had given. It took some time, and they were nearly late for Church, but not quite.

If Mademoiselle de Lavalette had been looking out of her window at a certain moment she would have been exceedingly surprised, not only by the transformation of Madame Clifford and *la petite bête* from church mice into visions, but still more by the sight of their companion.

But hot rage and cold disappointment had given her a bad night.

She had expected a guest for dinner. She had put on her prettiest frock, and had forbidden her mother the Comtesse to paint. She had ordered champagne, an extra entrée, and a bunch of flowers for the table. Yet the guest had neither come nor sent an excuse. She had stopped in the house all the evening, thinking that he might have been detained by an accident to his automobile; but the hours had dragged on emptily. Nothing happened except a bad headache, and a quarrel with her mother, who was ungratefully inclined to be sarcastic at her expense.

Half the night Mademoiselle had lain awake, wondering why the bird had not come hopping into the trap; and through the other half she had wondered anxiously if the bird would come to-morrow, with excuses which she might graciously accept. At last she had fallen asleep and dreamed ecstatic dreams about diamond necklaces and thousand franc notes. When the procession of three left the Beau Soleil on its way to the English Church, strings of diamonds were still being drawn through Mademoiselle's head, charming though wreathed with patent curling pins.

It was half past eleven when she was waked by the Comtesse ringing for *petits pains* and chocolate. A toilette was hastily made, without too much time being wasted on water; and Mademoiselle,—all in black and white this morning, like a *jeune fille* in second mourning,—hurried out to walk on the terrace at the fashionable hour. If she did not find the truant there, she said to herself, she would go into the Casino; for he was sure to be in one place or the other at this time of day, even though it was Christmas.

She walked a little, but not much; for her high-heeled shoes were tight, and made her feel even more annoyed with the world and everyone in it—except herself—than she had been before she started. Presently she sat down on one of the green benches, and arranged a "peace on earth, goodwill to men" expression which pinched her lips almost as painfully as her shoes pinched her toes. She wore it unremittingly, nevertheless, even though many of the women who passed her, walking on the terrace, were prettier and younger and better dressed than she, and—more grievous still—were accompanied by agreeable looking men, while she sat alone scarcely glanced at by the promenaders.

She had just begun to think that she had better try the Casino, when down the steps from the upper terrace came three figures. There was something familiar about them all, but to see them together made them more than strange. Besides, the two she knew best were strange in another way. Their habit was to be shabby, though neat; now, there was no one on the terrace as beautifully dressed as this tall young woman and the slim little girl. No, it couldn't be Madame Clifford and her *petit choux*; and yet—and yet—as they came nearer, near enough for Mademoiselle to recognise the man with them, she felt a horrid sensation as if something which she called her heart were dropping out of her bosom from sheer heaviness, leaving a vacuum.

They came nearer, near enough for Mademoiselle to recognize the man with them. .

—Rosemary.

Hardly knowing what she did, she sprang up from her bench while they were still far off, and began walking towards them. There was a queer, singing noise in her head, and a feeling as if the skin were too tightly stretched across her forehead. Still, she smiled, and winked her long lashes to keep her eyes moist and soft.

The sun was on Evelyn Clifford's hair, burnishing it to a halo of gold under the white hat. She looked radiantly beautiful, and as happy as if her soul were singing a Christmas Carol. On the face of Hugh Egerton was a look which no woman could mistake, least of all such a woman as Julie de Lavalette; and it was not for her, never would be for her.

Now she knew why her expected guest had not come last night, or remembered to send an excuse. Sick with jealousy and spite, she bowed as she passed, trying to look eighteen, and tenderly reproachful.

Her bow was returned, indifferently by Evelyn, but by Hugh with eyes of steel, and a mouth of bronze. If he had cut her, he would have shown less contempt than in that stiff raising of the hat.

Julie turned and walked straight down to the Condamine, forgetting that her shoes were tight.

THE LAST WORD OF MADEMOISELLE

Rosemary chose the toys for the children of the rock village, and then the "picnic" began.

The car whizzed them up the zigzag road to La Turbie, while the noon sunshine still gilded Caesar's Trophy. They lunched in the Moorish restaurant, and then sped on along the Upper Corniche, with a white sea of snow mountains billowing away to the right, and a sea of sapphire spreading to the horizon, on their left.

Out from orange groves and olives they saw the hill of Éze rising like a horn; while on its almost pointed apex, the old town hung like some carved fetish, to keep away the witches.

The car swooped down, and up again; but half way up the rocky horn the wide white road turned into a stone paved mule path, old as the Romans. Evelyn and Rosemary climbed hand in hand, singing a Christmas carol, while Hugh carried the two huge baskets filled with toys, and sweets in little packets.

Some small sentinel perched on high (perhaps hidden among the ruins of that fortress-castle where once the temple of Isis stood) must have spied the odd procession; for as the tall white girl and the little blue one, with the brown young man, reached the last step of the steep mule path, a tidal wave of children swept down upon them, out from the mystery of dark tunnelled streets.

Such eyes were never seen as those that gleamed at the new comers, great with surprise and wonder; eyes of brown velvet with diamonds shining through; eyes like black wells, with mirrored stars in their unfathomed depths; eyes of wild deer; eyes of fierce Saracens; eyes of baby saints, all set in small bronze faces clear-cut as the profiles on ancient Roman coins.

"Bella Madonna, bella Madonna!" piped a tiny voice, and forty other voices caught up the adoring cry.

The brown children of the old rock village had poured down from their high eyrie to bombard the strangers from the world below; to stare, to beg, to laugh, to lisp out strange epithets in their crude *patois*; but at sight of the wonderful white lady and her gold-haired child they crowded back upon each other, hushed after their first cry into awed admiration for visitants from another world.

Few tourists climbed to their dark fastness, and of those who came none had ever shone with such blinding radiance of white and gold.

It was certain that the lovely lady was none other than the Madonna herself, and the child she had brought was some baby angel. The man alone was mortal. He had perhaps been bidden to show la bella Madonna the way to Éze.

Rosemary, shy but happy, began giving out the toys, diving with both hands at once into the baskets which the fairy father held. Trumpets, bags of marbles, tops and furry animals for the boys, according to their age; (oh, Rosemary was a good judge, and never hesitated once!) Dolls for the girls, dolls by the dozen, dolls by the legion; and sweets for all.

As the amazed children received their gifts, they fell respectfully back, as if they had received an order to give place to their companions, and others came forward, open mouthed, large eyed, ready to fall upon their knees if but one of their number should set an example.

Still there were toys left, toys in abundance; the wondrous benefactors passed slowly on, always going up, up into the huddled village streets—tunnelled in rock or arched with stone, where eager, astonished faces peered from the mystery of shadowed doorways, and the hum of joy and admiration swelled to a sound like the murmur of the sea.

Of grown folk there were not many. A few mothers with brown babies in their arms; a few mumbling crones, and bent old men with faces like strange masks; but the flow of children never ceased.

As the children of Hamlin followed the Pied Piper to the sea, so the black browed children of Éze followed the Christmas visitors from crooked street to crooked street, up to the castle ruins and back again. They did not shout as they took their gifts; but still the murmur ran from mouth to mouth: "Bella Madonna, bella Madonna."

At the end of an enchanted hour, when there was not a child in Éze who had not both hands full, the benefactors turned to go, with empty baskets. Massed on the plateau above the mule-path, the whole population of the village stood to watch them down the steep descent. As they went, the church bells of Éze boomed out, calling all pious souls, young and old, to vespers; and as if the loosened tongues of the bells loosened also the tongues of the children, at last there arose a cry.

"Come again, Bella Madonna and little angel, come again. We shall pray to see you next Christmas Day, Bella Madonna and little angel. Don't forget, next Christmas Day."

"I'm perfectly happy, dearest," said Rosemary, when once more they sat in the car, spinning back from the shaded eyrie to the fair world where the sunshine lay.

The others did not speak, but the same thought was in their hearts.

When you are positively bursting with happiness the best outlet for the surplus quantity is to benefit somebody else; and there is no time like Christmas for a successful experiment.

"What else can we do for somebody?" asked Hugh.

"There's Jane," suggested Rosemary. "I told her this morning how I went out and found a father, and she said Pooh, he was all in my eye; and besides she'd never heard of fathers growing on blackberry bushes. But if we bought her a present, and you gave it to her yourself, she'd have to believe in you."

"I shan't feel I have a sure hold on existence until she does," said Hugh. "Let's buy her something without the loss of a moment."

So they bought Jane a ring, which Rosemary chose herself after mature deliberation, and with due regard to the recipient's somewhat pronounced taste in colours.

"She admires red and green together more than anything," said the child, "and I want her to have what she really likes, because if it hadn't been for her I shouldn't have known Christmas Eve was the time to search for fathers. Just supposing somebody else had gone out and snapped him up instead of me!"

As a matter of fact somebody else had gone out, and had come very near indeed to snapping him up; but there are things which do not bear thinking of. It was Hugh's firm conviction that Destiny and not Jane, had flung Rosemary in front of his motor; but Destiny could not be rewarded and Jane could.

Rosemary would be satisfied with nothing less than a formal presentation; and that the ceremony might be gone through without delay, the car was directed towards the Condamine. As they neared the street of the Hotel Pension Beau Soleil, a cab came jingling round the corner.

It was occupied by two ladies who sat half buried in travelling bags, rugs, baskets, and shawl straps, such as women who are not of the Anglo Saxon races love. A tiny motorphobe in the shape of a black Pomeranian yapped viciously at the automobile as the vehicles passed each other; and though the ladies—one stout, the other slim—were thickly veiled, Rosemary cried out, "Oh, it's the Comtesse and Mademoiselle. They must be going away."

Hugh said nothing, but his silence was eloquent to Evelyn, who knew now the whole story of the girl with the soft eyes. Both were pleased that this was the last of her; but neither quite knew Mademoiselle de Lavalette. She had been busy with other matters besides her packing, while la bella Madonna and her suite were collecting adorers on the heights of Éze.

Evelyn and Rosemary disappeared to take off their hats before the grand presentation ceremony should begin, and Hugh had begun to occupy the time of their absence by lighting the fire with pine cones, when a cry from the beloved voice called him to the room adjoining.

The door was open, and the woman and the child stood dumbfounded and overwhelmed in a scene of incredible desolation.

The air was acrid with the smell of burning. Blouses, pink and green, and cream, and blue, were stirred into a seething mass in the fireplace, as in a witch's cauldron, their fluffy laces burnt and blackened. Chiffon fichus torn in ribbons strewed the carpet. An ivory fan had been trampled into fragments on the hearth-rug, and a snow-storm of feathers from a white boa had drifted over the furniture. On the wash-stand a spangled white tulle hat lay drowning in a basin half full of water.

Their fluffy laces burnt and blackened. Chiffon fichus torn in ribbons strewed the carpet.

—*Rosemary.*

It was a sight to turn the brain of Madame in the magasin of smart "confections," nor would the presiding genius of the toy shop have gone scathless, for Rosemary's possessions had not been spared by the cyclone.

Dolls had lost their wigs, their arms, their legs; and beautiful blue eyes had been poked into far recesses of porcelain heads, with ruthless scissors. Little dresses of silk and satin had been flung to feed the flames which devoured ill-starred blouses; picture books had made fine kindlings; and that proud and stately mansion which might have afforded shelter to many dolls had collapsed as if shattered by a cyclone.

"Oh, Angel, is it some dreadful dream?" wailed Rosemary; and Evelyn found no answer. But Hugh had pounced upon a card pinned on the window curtain; and as he held it out, in eloquent silence, she read aloud over his shoulder; "Compliments of Mademoiselle de Lavalette."

At the end of the first shocked instant, they both laughed wildly, desperately. It was the only thing to do.

"After all," gasped Evelyn, "she has paid me back—what she owed me,—and Rosemary."

"She's given me the pleasure of making Christmas come all over again, to-morrow, that's all," said Hugh. "Women are strange. Thank heaven, *she* has vanished."

"But nothing matters—at least not much," said Rosemary, smiling through her tears, "since you're not going to vanish, fairy father."

THE END

Booksophile
Your Local Online Bookstore

Buy Books Online from
www.Booksophile.com

Explore our collection of books written in various languages and uncommon topics from different parts of the world, including history, art and culture, poems, autobiography and bibliographies, cooking, action & adventure, world war, fiction, science, and law.

Add to your bookshelf or gift to another lover of books - first editions of some of the most celebrated books ever published. From classic literature to bestsellers, you will find many first editions that were presumed to be out-of-print.

Free shipping globally for orders worth US$ 100.00.

Use code "Shop_10" to avail additional 10% on first order.

Visit today
www.booksophile.com

www.ingramcontent.com/pod-product-compliance
Lightning Source LLC
Chambersburg PA
CBHW031153090426
42738CB00008B/1314